Why I Was Late for School Again

By Dan Greenburg
Illustrated by Deborah Zemke

Chapter 1

"Danny, do you see what time it is?" Mom yelled. "It's 8:30! You have thirty minutes to get to school before the bell!"

"I'm just putting on my jacket and tying my shoes!" I shouted. "If you want, I could leave without putting on my jacket and tying my shoes — is that what you want?"

"If you're late one more time, young man, I'll have to go in to see Mrs. Finkelplotz! Is that what *you* want?"

Somewhere in the background my baby sister was screaming.

"Don't worry, Mom!" I shouted. "You won't have to go in to see Mrs. Finkelplotz. "I have thirty minutes to get there on time — there's no way I could be late today! Oh, where did you put my lunch money?"

"Right on the table by the door where I always put it. Now will you please get out of here already?"

"I am out of here, O.K.?" I shouted. "I'm history!"

Why do my mom and I always scream at each other when it's time for me to leave for school? Why is it so hard for me to leave the house? Maybe it's because really frightening things happen to me on the way to school.

My name is Danny. I'm in the fourth grade at the Stewart School in Chicago.

I get beat up a lot by the fourth grade bully. That's not too much fun. But it's better than getting beat up by the fifth grade bully, who hits harder. But the really scary stuff doesn't happen at school, like you think it would. It happens on the way.

My teacher, Mrs. Finkelplotz, gets mad when I'm late for school, and that's not fair. O.K., I'm late a lot, I admit it. But the problem is, she doesn't believe my excuses when I'm late. I know the things that happen to me sound pretty far out, but they really do happen.

I'm not a liar. Is it my fault weird things happen to me on the way to school? Is it my fault they make me late? Nobody ever believes me when I explain why I was late for school. Not even my mom or dad.

Maybe *you* will. Just listen, O.K.? Then *you* decide.

Chapter 2

When I got outside, it was so foggy, it was like walking through clouds. I could barely see the houses right across the street. I tried not to take the route to school that goes past the graveyard near my house, but I messed up. I must have gotten lost in the fog.

Before I knew it, I was walking past rows and rows and rows of graves. Everything was gray and moist and creepy looking. Most of the old gravestones were covered with greenish black mold.

The fog smelled like an old beach house that hadn't been lived in for years, a house that was always damp, a house where people had died. The fog covered me like a wet blanket that seeped into my eyes and ears and mouth. It creeped me out that I was breathing in the same fog that was covering graves where dead people were buried and rotting.

I'm nine years old, but walking past this graveyard always spooks me. The farther I walked, the creepier it felt. I imagined the graves bursting open and dead guys crawling out of them. What would I do if that happened? I mean, I admit that kind of thing doesn't happen too often, but what if it happened to me? What would I do?

I turned around and started to go back the way I came. But I hadn't got far when I saw something I wish I hadn't.

A bunch of spooky-looking people were coming toward me in the mist. They were walking stiffly, like their legs were sore from doing way too many deep knee bends in gym class. When they got closer, I saw that they had no shoes.

Their clothes were black and peeling away in long strips. Their skin was gray and awful looking, and it was peeling away in long strips, too. Their eyes were completely white.

I tried not to act scared.

"W-who are you?" I asked.

"WE ARE THE UN-DEAD," moaned the tallest one.

O.K., I thought, so they're the un-dead. That might not be as bad as it sounds. Mrs. Finkelplotz taught us that UN means NOT. So UN-dead might mean NOT-dead. As in Alive.

"I guess you could say that I am un-dead, too," I said.

"REALLY?" said the tallest one. He seemed to be their leader. "YOU MEAN YOU ARE A ZOMBIE, TOO?"

Uh-oh. Maybe un-dead wasn't such a great thing to be after all.

Chapter 3

"Y-you mean you guys are zombies?" I asked.

"YES, ZOMBIES," said the zombie leader. "HUNGRY ZOMBIES. ZOMBIES WHO HAVE NOT EATEN IN MORE THAN EIGHTY YEARS."

Wow, eighty years. I felt sorry for them. I know how hungry I get when I haven't eaten for even eighty minutes. Just thinking about that would make me hungry now if I didn't feel like puking all over my shoes.

Here's a funny thing, though. When you're feeling sorry for somebody, it makes you less afraid of them. That's kind of how I felt about the zombies.

I looked at my watch. It was 8:40. I still had

twenty minutes to get to school before the 9:00 late bell.

"ZOMBIES EAT HUMAN BRAINS," explained the head zombie. "CAN YOU TELL US WHERE TO FIND SOME DELICIOUS HUMAN BRAINS?"

"Hmm," I said. "Human brains, human brains. You know, that's a tough one."

I tried to think of a place around the graveyard that served human brains, but I couldn't.

"How about a nice pizza instead?" I offered.

"WHAT IS PIZZA?" asked the littlest zombie.

He was cute, in a sickening kind of way. He had a red buzzcut on the parts of his head that still had skin on it. And he had freckles, although his cheeks were rotting so badly you could see his skull underneath.

O.K., maybe he wasn't cute after all.

"IS THIS PIZZA YOU SPEAK ABOUT

ANYTHING LIKE HUMAN BRAINS?" asked the head zombie.

"No, not exactly," I said.

"IF IT IS NOT EXACTLY LIKE HUMAN BRAINS, IS IT QUITE SIMILAR TO HUMAN BRAINS?" pressed the head zombie.

"I don't think pizza is even a little bit similar to human brains," I said. "Although, to tell you the truth, I can't really remember the last time I tasted human brains."

"PERHAPS YOU CAN TELL US WHAT PIZZA IS LIKE," suggested a tall zombie with rotting teeth.

"Sure," I said. "Well, it's got cheese and crust and tomato sauce. And you can put other stuff on top of it, too. Like mushrooms, which I love. Or like anchovies, which I hate. And…well, it's kind of hard to describe."

"EVEN THOUGH IT DOES NOT TASTE LIKE HUMAN BRAINS, IS PIZZA DELICIOUS?" asked the head zombie.

"Oh, definitely," I assured him. "Pizza is definitely delicious. If you want to know the truth, I personally think pizza is even more delicious than human brains. But that's just me."

"ARE THERE PLACES AROUND HERE THAT SERVE THIS PIZZA?" asked the head zombie. "FRANKLY, WE ARE SO HUNGRY NOW, WE COULD EAT TOMBSTONES."

"Well, let me think." I scratched my head. "There's an Original Rocco's Pizza Parlor not far from here. Do you know Original Rocco's?"

"NO," he said.

"O.K., I'll direct you. What you do is, you walk two blocks north. Then you turn left at the traffic light. That's Montrose. Then you walk one block east. That's Broadway. And there it is. Original Rocco's. You can't miss it."

"IT SOUNDS CONFUSING," said the head zombie. "ZOMBIES HAVE NO SENSE OF DIRECTION. SOMETIMES WE GET LOST RIGHT IN THE MIDDLE OF THE GRAVEYARD."

"Really?" I asked.

"REALLY. SOMETIMES WE CANNOT EVEN FIND OUR WAY BACK TO OUR OWN GRAVES. WOULD YOU BELIEVE THAT?"

The zombies all laughed pretty hard at the idea of getting lost on the way back to their own graves.

So did I, just to be polite. I didn't actually think anything that happened in a graveyard was all that funny.

"Well," I said, "Original Rocco's is a famous place. If you get lost, just ask anybody where it is. They'll be glad to direct you."

"WE HAVE LIVED IN THIS GRAVEYARD FOR EIGHTY YEARS, BUT WE DO NOT KNOW THE NEIGHBORHOOD," explained the head zombie. "COULD YOU TAKE US TO THIS ORIGINAL ROCCO'S?"

"Normally, I'd love to." I tried to smile. "But I'm on my way to school and I'm already late. If I take you to Original Rocco's, I'll be even later. My teacher will be mad at me, and my mom will kill me."

"IF YOUR MOM KILLED YOU," said one of the zombies, "THEN YOU COULD HANG

OUT WITH US. WOULDN'T THAT BE FUN?"

"I'm sure it would be really cool." I tried to sound enthusiastic. "But when I said my mom will kill me, I didn't mean she will literally kill me. I just meant that she will be really mad at me, that's all."

"SO THEN WHAT WOULD SHE DO, JUST CHOP OFF YOUR ARMS OR WHAT?" asked the littlest zombie in a high squeaky voice.

"No, no, nothing like that," I yelped. "She would probably just yell at me. Anyway, the point is, I  can't be late to school again, so I can't take you to Original Rocco's. But hey, it's been great meeting you and everything. See you around."

I waved goodbye and turned to go.

16

"UNLESS YOU TAKE US TO ORIGINAL ROCCO'S," threatened the head zombie, "WE SHALL BE FORCED TO EAT YOU."

Yikes! I turned around and ran down the block like a madman. I'm a pretty fast runner for a kid my age and definitely faster than zombies walking in that stiff-legged walk of theirs, so pretty soon I was yards ahead of them. As long as I kept running, I would probably be O.K. And as long as I stayed away from that graveyard.

Chapter 4

I kept running till I was way past the grave-yard. Ahead of me was Belmont Harbor. As I ran past the harbor, I shot a fast look at the boats. I always love looking at the boats in Belmont Harbor. Breathing in the seawater beach smell. Hearing the waves slap against the hulls and the ropes clang against the masts.

Someone behind me yelled, "Ahoy there!"

I turned around. I saw a big guy with a bushy black beard. He had on old-fashioned clothes like you see in history books. He wore a black eye patch and a funny hat. I figured he was a homeless man.

"Could ye spare a few coins for an old salt?" he

asked in a weird accent.

I kept running, but I slowed down to be polite.

"Thanks, but I don't need any old salt," I said. "My mom buys new salt at the A&P."

He started running alongside me to continue the conversation.

"An old salt means an old sailor," he explained. "Would ye be havin' any money on ye for an old sailor, lad?"

"No, sir," I said. "All I have is my lunch money."

"Lunch money?" he asked. "Very well then, let's have it. I'd like some lunch."

He held out his hand.

I feel bad for homeless people, I really do. But I needed my lunch money for MY lunch.

"I'm sorry, sir." I started to run faster. "I need this money to buy lunch at school today."

This made him angry. He muttered something under his breath. Then he pulled out the biggest sword I've ever seen.

A sword! Now do you see why I'm scared to leave the house every morning?

I sped up and pulled away from him. As I said before, I'm a pretty fast runner. Soon I had left the homeless man, if that's what he was, far behind me.

Chapter 5

When I left Belmont Harbor, I took a gravel path through Lincoln Park that was another short-cut to school. The gravel path took me to a stream with a little bridge over it. I could hear the stream gurgling under the bridge. The bridge was made out of logs. It looked like it had been put together by somebody who learned bridge-building from a book written in a foreign language.

On the bridge was a sign: "TOLL BRIDGE, PAY TOLL." The sign didn't say how much the toll was, and I didn't see a toll taker. I started to walk across the bridge.

That's when I heard a big splash. A nasty little

creature jumped out from where she'd been hiding and pulled herself up onto the bridge with a grunt. She stood there, dripping water and blocking my path.

The creature had a single strand of a pony tail sprouting from her bald head. She had yellow skin, lots of brown warts, gigantic hairy ears, and a nose like a giant salami.

"Hey," I yelled, "get out of my way!"

"Didn't you see the sign?" demanded the creature.

"Yeah, it says 'Toll Bridge, Pay Toll.'"

"No," said the creature. "It says 'TROLL BRIDGE, PAY TROLL.' I'm the troll. Pay me my toll."

"How much is your toll?" I asked.

"Eighty thousand dollars," the troll answered.

"Eighty thousand dollars!" I yelped. "Where would I get eighty thousand dollars? All I have is my lunch money."

"Is your lunch money eighty thousand dollars?" she asked.

"No, three dollars," I admitted.

"Oh," said the troll. "Well, if you can't pay the toll, then grant me a wish."

"Grant you a wish? What is your wish?" I asked.

"I want to be a rock star," insisted the troll. "A beautiful rock star with long flowing hair and a sparkly shirt."

"Look," I explained, "I'm not a genie. . . I'm a kid on his way to school. I can't grant wishes."

"If you don't grant my wish," whined the troll, "then how will I become a rock star?"

"How should I know?" I shrugged. "Form a garage band with other trolls. Practice a lot. Enter a talent contest or something. Do you play the guitar?"

"Yes, but I only know one chord," moaned the troll.

"Well, are you an amazing drummer?"

"I couldn't tell you which end to hold a drumstick," groaned the troll.

"Do you sing?"

"My voice sounds like a pig with whooping cough," rasped the troll.

"Then how were you planning to become a rock star?"

"By getting somebody to grant me a magic

wish," argued the troll.

"Well, I don't think you can find anyone to do that," I said. "At least not me."

"Then you can't cross my bridge," the troll insisted.

"Fine. I'll go back the way I came," I answered.

"After you've already crossed half my bridge?" she griped.

"Yeah."

"Then give me half my toll," the troll yelled. "Give me forty thousand dollars!"

"I don't have forty thousand dollars!" I shouted.

"Then I won't let you pass." The troll crossed her arms and glared at me.

Chapter 6

"Isn't there anything else I can give you as a toll?" I asked.

"I don't know," said the troll. "Do you have any magic jellybeans in assorted flavors?"

"No."

"A Harley-Davidson motorcycle with a padded seat?"

"No."

"How about a pair of budgies who say 'Hello, sweetheart, give me a kiss'?"

"I'm afraid not," I said.

The troll looked pretty disappointed.

"Then could you at least take a thorn out of my paw?" she asked.

"I don't know. Do you really have a thorn in your paw?"

"Yes," she groaned.

"Let me see it."

The troll held out her paw.

Her paw was huge. It had five nasty-looking curvy claws. They were a dirty yellow color, and they looked rough and cracked. Under each claw was a leathery pad. Sticking out of the middle pad was a tiny thorn.

"Do you see the thorn?" asked the troll.

"I see it."

"It really hurts me," whined the troll.

She started to cry. That made me sad. Not as bad as if my baby sister was crying but sad enough to be really uncomfortable.

"Please don't cry," I said.

"Why not?"

"Because. It makes me sad," I said. "Trolls aren't supposed to cry."

"Are you an expert on trolls?" She sniffled.

"No," I admitted.

"Then don't tell me trolls don't cry. If you can remove that thorn, I'll be your friend forever."

"Really? And what if I can't?"

"If you can't," threatened the troll, "I'll chew your hand off."

I didn't like the way this was going. I looked at my watch. It was 9:00 and I was now officially late for school. But if I could remove the thorn fast and then run really hard, I might still make it to school by 9:15, which would be late, but not so late that I'd have to go to the principal's office or that my mom would have to go and see Mrs. Finkleplotz.

"Do you have a name?" I asked.

"Of course I have a name," scoffed the troll. "It's Throg."

"Throg, my name is Danny. I'll be glad to try and remove the thorn from your paw. But if I can't do it, I don't want you to chew my hand off."

"I can't help it," said Throg. "That's what trolls do. They chew people's hands off. That's the rule. So you better get it out."

Chapter 7

I held Throg's paw with one hand. With the other I tried to grab the thorn between my fingernails.

Twice I almost had it. Twice it slipped away.

"This is taking too long," moaned Throg. "Are you almost done?"

"I will be if I can just hang onto that thorn," I said.

"What's taking so long?" she sniveled.

"I can't get a grip on it."

"You better get a grip soon," groaned Throg. "I feel a good chew coming on."

"You're making me nervous," I said. "And if I'm nervous, it's harder to do this."

I grabbed at the thorn again. I got a grip on it again. This time it didn't slip away.

I pulled.

The thorn came out, but it was longer than I thought. A lot longer than I thought.

The more I pulled, the more came out.

It was no longer a thorn. It was more like a long piece of string. A very long piece of string.

"What are you doing there?" Throg howled.

"Pulling out your thorn," I said. "It's attached to a long piece of string."

"String?" Throg repeated. "What's string doing in my paw?"

"I don't know," I said.

I pulled harder.

Throg screamed.

"What's wrong?" I asked.

"What's wrong?" she bellowed. "Look at my other paw!"

I looked at her other paw. It had just disappeared into her wrist!

"Uh-oh," I gulped.

"What's happening to me?" Throg shrieked.

"I don't know, Throg," I said. "Your paws seem

to be attached to each other by a long string. Like mittens on a little kid's snowsuit. Pulling on one seems to be yanking the other into your wrist."

"Then stop!" Throg screamed. "I want my paw back!"

"Right," I agreed.

I stopped pulling on the string. I took Throg's other arm and looked into the end of it. It was hollow. It was like looking into the end of a pipe. I could see her other paw. It was inside her arm, about six inches away. I tried to stick my hand inside her hollow arm. It felt moist and clammy.

"Get your hand out of my arm!" Throg shrieked. "It hurts!"

"Do you want your paw back or don't you?" I asked.

"Do I want my paw back?" she yowled. "Of course I want my paw back!"

"Well, this is the only way we can get it back," I explained.

"Then do it," she moaned.

"What if it hurts?" I wanted to be sure.

"If it hurts, I'll bite you," she growled.

"That's not fair," I yelped.

"Trolls aren't fair," she said. "Trolls aren't supposed to be fair. Get my paw back or I'll bite you."

Chapter 8

I put my hand back inside her arm and tried to grab her paw.

At first I couldn't even reach it.

Then I reached it, but I couldn't get a grip on it.

Then I got a grip on it.

Then I pulled.

Her paw started coming out.

Very, very slowly at first.

Then faster.

Then it started coming out so fast, I couldn't stop it. Her paw came out way past the end of her wrist.

"Hey!" Throg screamed. "Stop before —"

As I watched in horror, Throg's head got sucked down into her neck.

I looked down into her neck. It was hollow.

About six inches into her neck, I could see the top of her pony tail and the tops of her huge ears.

Oh no! What had I done? Throg would really be angry at me now!

I had to pull her head out of her neck before she choked. But if I did that, wouldn't she bite me? Maybe it was better to leave her head stuck inside her neck. Then at least she couldn't bite me.

But then maybe she'd choke to death. I didn't want her to choke to death, even if she was a very nasty troll and she wasn't letting me cross her bridge.

What should I do?

Chapter 9

It was 9:15. I was already late, and it looked like I was going to be a lot later.

I had to do something, and I had to do it fast.

Just then I heard a sound: trip-trap, trip-trap. Somebody had just walked onto the troll's bridge. I looked to see who it was.

It was a goat. A billy goat had started across the bridge. Trip-trap, trip-trap. When he got up to where I was standing with the troll, he stopped.

"Get out of my way," said the billy goat in a gruff voice.

I thought that was pretty rude.

"Who do you think you are?" I asked.

"I think I'm First Billy Goat Gruff," he sneered. "I'm crossing this bridge to get to the hill on the other side where the grass is green and where I can grow big and fat. If you don't get out of my way, I'll butt you right into the water."

"What do you mean, get out of your way or you'll butt me into the water?" I asked.

"Not only you, but your stupid headless friend," said the billy goat.

"I heard that!" shouted the troll from inside her body. Her voice sounded all echoey like she was deep inside a well. "Don't think I can't hear you just because my head happens to be jammed down inside my body."

"Tell your stupid headless friend to get out of my way," ordered the billy goat.

"First of all," I said, "this headless person is not stupid. Second, she's not my friend. And third, even though she's not my friend, I already like her way better than you. Now get off this bridge or I'll…"

"You'll what?" demanded the billy goat.

"I'll call you bad names and make you cry," I said.

First Billy Goat Gruff thought this over.

"What would you call me?" he asked. He looked worried.

"I don't know," I admitted. "I might call you… Cow Tushy."

First Billy Goat Gruff burst into tears and ran off the bridge back in the direction he had come.

"I heard hoofbeats," called the troll. "Did the billy goat leave?"

"Yes," I said. "I threatened to call him a bad name."

"What name did you threaten to call him?" yelled the troll.

"Cow Tushy," I said.

"I don't care for bad language," bellowed the troll in her echoey voice. "If you're going to use words like Cow Tushy, I'm not going to let you cross my bridge. By the way, how are we doing on getting my head out of my body?"

"I was just trying to think of a way to do that when the billy goat arrived and interrupted me," I said.

"Well, you better get back to thinking," called the troll in her echoey voice. "I'm starting to feel chewy."

Chapter 10

I scratched my head and tried to figure out what to do about the troll's head. Maybe I should just forget about it and get to school before I was even later.

Just then I heard somebody else walk onto the bridge. Trip-trap, trip-trap. It was another billy goat, but this one was bigger than the first one.

When he got up to where I was standing with the troll, he stopped.

"Get out of my way," said the bigger billy goat.

Another rude goat.

"And who do you think you are?" I asked.

"I'm Bigger Billy Goat Gruff," he growled. "I'm

the big brother of the billy goat you may have seen a little while ago. I'm crossing this bridge to get to the hill on the other side where the grass is green and where I can grow big and fat. If you don't get out of my way, I'll be all over you like flies on a pile of poop."

"What do you mean, get out of your way or you'll be all over me like flies on a pile of poop? What kind of way is that to talk to somebody you just met?"

"I'll not only be all over you like flies on a pile of poop," sneered the billy goat, "I'll also be all over your ugly headless friend."

"First of all," I said, "you have no right to call this person ugly without seeing her head. Second, as I already explained to your brother, she's not my friend. And third, I already like her way better than you or your brother. Now get off this bridge, or I'll call you bad names and make you cry."

Bigger Billy Goat Gruff thought this over.

"Not that I care, but just out of curiosity, what would you call me?" he asked. He looked nervous.

"I don't know," I said. "I might call you... Marmalade Fart."

Bigger Billy Goat Gruff thought this over a minute. Then he burst into tears and galloped off the bridge back in the direction he had come.

"Did that one leave too?" howled the troll.

"Yes, he did," I said.

"What name did you call him?" asked the troll.

"Marmalade Fart," I said.

"Did I tell you I don't care for bad language or didn't I?" shouted the troll.

"I'm sorry. But that seems to be the only way to get billy goats off your bridge. So if I were you, I wouldn't be so cranky about what works. Now let's think of a way to get your head out of your body."

"You better think a lot faster than you've been

thinking," screeched the troll. "I'm getting pretty angry in here."

Chapter 11

Just then I heard somebody else get onto the bridge. TRIP-TRAP, TRIP-TRAP. It was another billy goat, but this one was way bigger than the other two. His hoofbeats were so heavy, they made the bridge shudder like a herd of elephants was trampling across it.

When he got up to where I was standing with the troll, he stopped.

"Get out of my way!" roared the even bigger billy goat in a very deep voice.

"And who do you think you are?" I asked.

"I'm Great Big Billy Goat Gruff," he bellowed. "I'm the biggest brother of the other two billy goats you may have seen earlier, and I am quite a bit stronger and scarier. I'm crossing this bridge to get to the hill on the other side where the grass is green and where I can use the cash machine. If you don't get out of my way, I'll stomp you flat, slap a slice of cheese on you, drop you onto a bun, and eat you like a cheeseburger."

"I've had it with all three of you billy goats gruff," I huffed. "If you don't turn right around and gallop off this bridge by the time I count to three, I'm going to call you bad names and make you cry."

"The very idea that you could call me a name that would make me cry is so funny, I could pee in my pants," scoffed Great Big Billy Goat Gruff. "If I wore pants, that is. Which I don't. Not that I'm the slightest bit worried, but just out of curiosity, what were you thinking of calling me?"

"I don't know," I said. "I might call you…Doody-Breath Goat Gruff."

Great Big Billy Goat Gruff looked at me for a moment. Then he suddenly burst into tears.

"That's not fair!" he sobbed.

He turned around and galloped back off the bridge.

"Did I just hear you call that person Doody-Breath Goat Gruff?" shouted the troll from way down inside her body.

"Yes," I said, "but it made him go away."

"Did I or did I not tell you I hate bad language?" yelled the troll.

"Well, yeah, you did, but—"

"Then get off my bridge!" screamed the troll. "Get your cow-tushy, marmalade-fart, doody-breath self off my bridge immediately, if not sooner!"

The troll began blindly swinging her fists around, trying to hit me. Since she couldn't see, it was easy for me to step out of the way and not get hit.

"Hang on a second, Throg," I said. "If I get off your bridge now, who's going to help you pull your head back out of your body?"

"I don't care about pulling my head back out of my body anymore!" screeched the troll. "I don't even need a head!"

"Really? What's going to happen when you want to blow your nose? What's going to happen when you want some chocolate ice cream with sprinkles and you have to pour it down your neck hole till you choke? What's going to happen when it rains, and the water collects inside your neck so deep that you can't breathe and you drown?"

"I don't know, I don't know, I don't know!" howled the troll.

She was crying and flailing her arms around. She was having a tantrum.

I had a choice. I could either do what she said and leave, or I could stay and help her out.

Even though she'd threatened to chew my hand off, I couldn't let her choke to death.

Or could I?

Then I knew what I had to do. Even if it meant I was going to get bitten.

Chapter 12

I reached both my hands down into the troll's neck.

With each hand I grabbed one of her huge ears.

I pulled.

Nothing happened. I pulled again.

Still nothing happened. I pulled a third time.

Throg's head popped out of her neck. It sounded

like a giant cork popping out of a bottle.

"Pheeeeeooooww!" Throg shouted.

Her face was bright red.

Her eyes were popping out of her head.

She looked really, really angry.

"You!" she yelled.

"Y-yes?" I said.

"You almost made me choke to death!" she accused.

"Yes, but I pulled your head out of your body before that happened," I said. "And I pulled a huge thorn out of your paw. And I got rid of three really rude billy goats. And I also saved your life."

Throg thought this over.

"I do wish you hadn't used words like Cow Tushy, Marmalade Fart, and Doody-Breath Goat Gruff," she said. "Trolls hate bad words. But it's true you saved my life."

She grabbed me and gave me a giant bear hug.

I don't know if you've ever been hugged by a troll. I mean, don't get me wrong, it's O.K., but it's also kind of slimy.

Anyway, Throg thanked me all over the place. And then she let me walk the rest of the way over her bridge without paying the eighty thousand dollars.

"We're now best friends for life," she promised. "Come over any time after school for video games and chocolate ice cream with sprinkles. What's your name again?"

"Danny," I said.

"O.K., Danny. When you come back, be sure the chocolate ice cream with sprinkles has chocolate whipped cream on top of it with at least one maraschino cherry."

"O.K.," I agreed. I had no idea what a maraschino cherry was, but I didn't have time to ask. It was probably a troll thing.

I looked at my watch. It was 9:35! I was thirty-five minutes late!

I raced off the bridge and down the gravel path through the park.

I must have taken a wrong turn somewhere, because before I knew it, I was back at Belmont Harbor. And standing right in my path was the homeless man with the big sword.

Chapter 13

"Oh, uh, hi there," I stammered. "We meet again."

The homeless man pulled out his sword and took a step in my direction.

"Start walkin', lad," he ordered.

"W-which way?" I asked.

"Straight ahead," he directed.

"How far?" I asked.

"Till I tell ye when to stop," he snarled.

I started walking. I was more scared of this guy than of the fifth-grade bully.

We walked out onto the docks, and he led me to this really old ship. It had three tall masts and about a thousand canvas sails. At the top of the tallest mast was a black flag. On the flag were a white skull and two crossed bones.

Uh-oh.

They call that the Jolly Roger. It's the pirate flag. Mrs. Finkelplotz told us that pirates disappeared from Chicago more than 200 years ago. Didn't these guys know that?

A bunch of sailors dressed like pirates came out onto the deck and gathered around us. I guess the homeless guy wasn't just a homeless guy but a pirate, too.

"Who have ye got there, Captain Pew?" asked one.

"Just a lad who wants to give us his lunch money," snorted Captain Pew.

"No, no," I said. "I can't do that, sir. I thought I explained. It's my lunch money. My mother gave me that money. If I lost it, she'd be really upset. She might even cry."

I don't know why I said that. My mother wouldn't cry if I lost my lunch money.

"Would your mum really cry if ye lost your lunch money?" asked a huge pirate.

He had a big scar running down the side of his face and a beard like a big reddish-orange bush. He was over seven feet tall, but even with the scar he had a really kind face.

"Yes, sir," I lied. "My mom often cries if I lose my lunch money." I figured it wouldn't be a good idea to change my story now.

"If the lad's mother is going to cry," said the reddish-orange-bearded pirate, "we can't take his lunch money away from him."

A few of the pirates agreed with the reddish-orange-bearded one.

"Tiny Tom is right!" they shouted. "Hear, hear!"

Apparently the huge reddish-orange-bearded

pirate was named Tiny Tom. There was grumbling among the men. Some agreed with Tiny Tom. Some didn't. I wanted to get more of them to agree with Tiny Tom.

"Maybe some of you men have mothers like I do," I wheedled. "I don't know about you, but it makes me sad to see my mother cry."

The grumbling grew louder.

"The lad is right!" shouted a man with a rusty steel hook instead of a left hand. "I saw my old mum cry once. It darn near broke my heart!"

"Same thing happened to me!" yelled a man with a wooden fence post for a leg. "When I saw my old mum cry, I got so sad it made me puke all over the floor!"

Some of the pirates started sniffling. Some were dabbing at their eyes with handkerchiefs.

I thought they must be pretty kind people to get so upset about their moms crying.

"What kind of pirates are ye!" demanded Captain Pew. "Havin' your hearts broke and pukin' when your mums cry? Have ye totally lost your blinkin' minds or what?"

Captain Pew grabbed me roughly.

"Give me your blinkin' lunch money!" he hissed.

"Captain Pew," I said, "I believe I already explained why I can't give you —"

"Give me your blinkin' lunch money if ye want to keep your blinkin' head on your blinkin' shoulders!" he screamed.

Chapter 14

I quickly handed Captain Pew my lunch money. I was scared but really angry.

The pirates grew very quiet. Was it possible they didn't like what Captain Pew had done to me?

That gave me an idea.

"Did you see that?" I asked the pirates. "Did you see what your captain just did there? He doesn't mind making my mother cry! He probably wouldn't mind making your mothers cry, either!"

"Give the lad his blinkin' lunch money!" shouted Tiny Tom.

"Give it back to him!" yelled a pirate with a purple parrot on her shoulder.

"Braack!" screeched the parrot. "Give it back! Give it back!"

"Not on your blinkin' life!" screamed Captain Pew.

"Is this the kind of man you want to lead you?" I shouted. "A man who would make your mothers cry?"

"No! No!" chanted the pirates.

"Then maybe you need to choose a better leader!" I urged.

"He's right!" they yelled. "We need a better leader! Let's mutiny!"

Mrs. Finkelplotz taught us that a mutiny means the sailors take control of the ship away from their captain. I don't know why I was being braver with the pirates than I am with the fifth-grade bully. Maybe because the fifth-grade bully does things like twist my arm behind my back and make me kiss the front door of the school with everybody watching, and the pirates didn't.

The men surrounded Captain Pew and locked him up in heavy, clangy chains. Then they gave me back my lunch money. I was pretty surprised.

"Thanks, mateys." I smiled. "I appreciate that."

"Anything to keep your mum from crying," said Tiny Tom. "What's your name, lad?"

"Danny."

"How old are ye, Danny?"

"Nine, sir."

"You know, Danny," he said, "we shall be needin' a new captain now. One who respects mothers."

"Great idea, Tiny Tom," I said.

"How would you like to be our new captain, Danny?"

Chapter 15

"Yeah! Danny for captain!" the pirates shouted. "Danny for captain!" They started cheering.

"Braaack!" screeched the parrot. "Danny for captain! Danny for captain!"

"Wow," I said. Would that be cool or what?

I never thought about becoming a pirate before, much less a pirate captain. It sure was an interesting idea. If I became a pirate captain, I would never have to do any homework ever again. If I became a pirate captain, I'd never have to worry about being late for school ever again.

If I became a pirate captain, I'd never get beaten up by the fifth-grade bully. If I became the pirate captain, I could take my pirates back to

Stewart School around lunch time and have them beat up the fifth-grade bully. He's pretty tough, but not as tough as a pirate crew.

If I became the pirate captain, my mom and dad would miss me and be sad. But it would serve them right for giving my baby sister my big bedroom and moving me into the small, back bedroom. They definitely love her more than me. They're always fussing over her. But if I became a pirate captain, my mom and dad would probably really miss me and be really sad. They might even cry. I'd like to see that.

No, I wouldn't. It would make me too sad to see my mom and dad cry, even if they love my baby sister more than me.

"Listen, guys, I'm really flattered," I said. "But I'm afraid I can't accept."

"Why not?" asked Tiny Tom. He looked disappointed.

"Well, first of all," I admitted, "I don't know anything about being a pirate captain."

"We could teach you," offered Tiny Tom.

"Second," I said, "I can't leave my mom and dad and my baby sister."

"We left our families," rasped the man with the hook for a hand.

"And third," I said, "as much as I'd like to, I really can't leave school. Which is, by the way, where I'm supposed to be right now."

"Awww," groaned the pirates.

"Why can't ye leave school, lad?" asked Tiny Tom.

"Well, if I left school, I wouldn't be able to go to college, get a good job, buy a house, get married and all that stuff you're supposed to do. But you know who'd be a great captain for you? Tiny Tom."

"Tiny Tom! Tiny Tom!" they began to chant. "Tiny Tom for captain!"

"How many of you want Tiny Tom to be your new captain?" I asked.

The pirates cheered really loudly.

"How many don't want Tiny Tom to be your new captain?" I shouted.

"I don't!" yelled Captain Pew.

The pirates all booed.

"It looks like you just voted yourself a new captain," I said. "Congratulations, Tiny Tom!"

Chapter 16

Everybody cheered. Everybody except Captain Pew, of course.

"What shall we do with Captain Pew, lads?" asked Tiny Tom.

"Make him walk the plank!" they roared together.

"Braaack!" screeched the parrot. "Walk the plank! Walk the plank!"

I remembered Mrs. Finkelplotz said walking the plank was when pirates made somebody walk off the end of a long wooden plank and fall into the water and drown. I didn't much like Captain Pew, but I didn't want to see him drown.

"Please don't make Captain Pew walk the

plank," I begged. "He's sorry he took my lunch money."

"I am not sorry I took yer blinkin' lunch money," snarled Captain Pew, rattling his chains. "What makes ye think I'm sorry?"

I ignored him. He was only making it tougher on himself. If the pirates had put me in chains, I sure wouldn't be blabbing about how I wasn't sorry I'd taken any blinkin' lunch money.

"Now that you're Captain, Tiny Tom," I suggested, "maybe you should make a rule that you guys won't take money from anybody who has a mother."

"That's the stupidest blinkin' thing I ever heard!" snapped Captain Pew. "Everybody has a blinkin' mother. If we can't take money from anybody who has a mother, how can we be pirates?"

"I don't know," I admitted. "Maybe you

shouldn't be pirates anymore."

The pirates gasped at this idea.

"Beggin' your pardon, Danny," said Tiny Tom, "but if we aren't pirates anymore, how would we earn a living? We do have to earn a living, you know."

"I know you do," I agreed. "Well, let me think about that."

How would they earn a living if they couldn't be pirates anymore?

"Maybe you could drive buses for the city of Chicago," I suggested.

"We are pirates of the sea, Danny," said Tiny Tom. "What do we know of buses?"

"O.K. Driving buses for the city of Chicago might not be the answer for men of the sea. Well then, maybe you could take tourists on sight-seeing cruises. Like along the Chicago waterfront."

"Could we make any money doing that?" asked the pirate with the parrot on her shoulder.

"Are you kidding me?" I grinned. "Taking tourists on sight-seeing cruises? You could make lots of money doing that, tons of money. More money than you could by being pirates."

"Sight-seeing cruises!" shouted the pirate with the parrot. "What a fine idea!"

"Fine idea! Fine idea! Braaack!" screeched the parrot.

All the pirates agreed that taking tourists on cruises of the Chicago waterfront was a fine idea.

"You know, guys," I said, "I am really late for school now. And as much fun as this has been, I have to go now."

I said goodbye to all the pirates.

Tiny Tom gave me a big bear hug. I really liked that guy, even though he smelled like he hadn't taken a shower in about thirty years.

I jumped off the pirate ship, raced down the dock, and then headed off in the direction of school.

Chapter 17

As I ran, I looked at my watch. It was now 10:30! I was an hour and a half late! I was a dead man for sure.

Speaking of dead men, the zombies I had run away from were now standing in the middle of the sidewalk directly ahead of me. Had I accidentally doubled back in the direction of the graveyard, or had they just wandered in the direction of the harbor while I was busy with the pirates?

I didn't know. Either way, they seemed pretty angry.

"WHY DID YOU RUN AWAY FROM US?" the zombie leader demanded. "WHY DID YOU

NOT TAKE US FOR PIZZA AT ORIGINAL ROCCO'S?"

"I'm really sorry, guys," I said. "But I'm so late for school, my life won't be worth a nickel if I don't race right over there."

"IF YOU DO NOT TAKE US TO ORIGINAL ROCCO'S FOR PIZZA IMMEDIATELY," threatened the zombie leader, "YOU WILL NO LONGER EVEN HAVE A LIFE. OR A NICKEL."

I decided to take the zombies to Original Rocco's.

It wasn't a long walk, but there was a problem getting them there. Zombies don't seem to understand about traffic lights. They crossed the street at Montrose when the light was red, and two cars honked at them. They crossed against the light at Broadway, too. A red Toyota side-swiped one of the zombies. The zombie's nose fell off.

The zombie looked angry. She punched the Toyota with her fist. It left a big hole in the hood. Steam boiled out of it.

The zombie ate both of the car's windshield wipers, its aerial, and its rearview mirror. The driver got out and ran away, leaving the car in the middle of the street. I would have done the same thing if a zombie started to eat my car.

The zombies ate the rest of the Toyota. When

they were done, only the engine block and a few wires were left.

"MMM." The littlest zombie smacked its lips. "THAT WAS DELICIOUS."

"I thought you guys only ate human brains," I said. "I didn't realize you ate cars."

"NOT JUST ANY CARS," explained the zombie leader. "ONLY RED TOYOTAS. THEY HAVE A WONDERFUL CHERRY FLAVOR."

"So I guess you guys aren't hungry anymore," I said hopefully.

"NO," said the zombie leader. "STILL HUNGRY. THAT WAS JUST A SNACK."

At least nothing else happened till we got to Original Rocco's.

The pizza guy behind the counter at Original Rocco's was wearing a white apron and a big white chef's hat.

"Hey," I greeted him. "How's it going?"

"I've had better days," he said. "What can I do for you guys this morning?"

He didn't look like he wanted to do anything for us guys this morning.

"We'd like six pizzas," I answered. "To eat here."

He shook his head. "Sorry, I can't serve you."

"Why not?" I asked.

He pointed to a big sign on the wall.

"Couldn't you make an exception here?" I insisted. "These guys are really hungry."

He shook his head again. "Nope. Sorry, no can

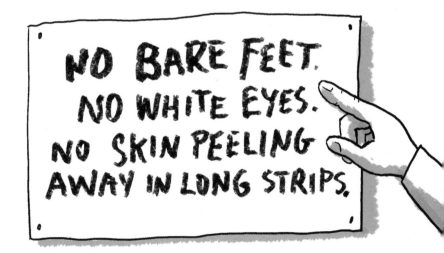

do. There are no exceptions."

"O.K., I'll tell you what," I offered. "We don't have to eat the pizzas here. We'll take them to go."

"Doesn't matter," he said. "I still can't serve you."

"Please?" I whined. "I'm begging you."

"Can't do it, buddy," he said. "Wish I could. I mean that sincerely."

"Look, these people are starving," I said. "They haven't eaten in eighty years. Except for one tiny red Toyota. Couldn't you just be a nice guy and sell them a few pizzas?"

"Hey, I don't make the rules around here, pal," he grumbled. "I just make pizza, you know what I'm saying?"

I didn't like this pizza guy at all. I also don't like people who call me "pal" and "buddy" when they don't even know my name.

I turned to the zombies.

"Bad news, guys," I said. "The pizza guy won't sell us any pizza."

"AWWW. WHY NOT?" asked the zombie leader.

"Oh, they have some silly rule here about not serving people who have bare feet, white eyes, or skin peeling away in long strips," I explained.

Just then I heard something hit the floor. One of the zombies had lost an arm. She picked it up, looked at it, and shrugged. Then she dunked it into the garbage bin.

"WE DO NOT NEED TO EAT PIZZA," roared the zombie leader. "WE WILL JUST EAT THE PIZZA GUY."

Chapter 18

"O.K., O.K.," said the pizza guy. "I was just kidding about not serving you. Ha ha."

"YOU WERE KIDDING US?" howled the zombie leader.

"Sure," stammered the pizza guy. "I can't believe you thought I was serious. What would you guys like on your pies?"

The zombies got together and talked it over.

"Hey," I said, "I'm really late for school. I'm going to go now, but you just tell the pizza guy what you want and he'll make it for you, O.K.?"

"YOU STAY HERE UNTIL WE GET OUR PIZZA," bellowed the zombie leader. "YOU MAKE SURE WE GET WHAT WE ORDER."

I sighed. "Whatever you say."

The head zombie turned back to the pizza guy.

"WE WANT SIX LARGE PIZZAS WITH PEPPERONI, SLUGS, AND EARTHWORMS," he ordered.

"Hey, pal, we got pepperoni, mushrooms, sausages, and anchovies," said the pizza guy. "That's it."

"NO SLUGS OR EARTHWORMS?" sobbed the littlest zombie.

He looked really disappointed. I was afraid he might cry, but then I realized he probably didn't even have tear ducts anymore.

"No," said the pizza guy. "No slugs or earthworms. Just pepperoni, mushrooms, sausages, and anchovies. Sorry."

I didn't think he was sorry. I walked over to the head zombie and whispered in his ear.

"If you want my opinion, the pizza guy is just

lazy. I don't think he feels like going to all the extra work of walking outside and digging up slugs and earthworms for six pies."

"THANK YOU FOR THE TIP," said the head zombie. "I APPRECIATE THE INFORMATION."

Then he walked right up close to the pizza guy.

"KNOW WHAT?" he shouted. "I CAN TWIST MY HEAD AROUND FOR THREE WHOLE TURNS BEFORE IT COMES OFF. HOW MANY CAN YOU TWIST YOURS?"

"I d-don't know," mumbled the pizza guy.

"OH, GOODY," snarled the head zombie, "LET'S FIND OUT."

He reached out toward the pizza guy's head.

"O.K., O.K.," said the pizza guy. "I was just kidding about not having slugs and earthworms. Ha ha."

"THEN YOU DO HAVE SLUGS AND EARTHWORMS?" hissed the head zombie.

"Of course we have slugs and earthworms," said the pizza guy. "This is Original Rocco's, right? I can't believe you thought I was serious."

The pizza guy got a shovel and a pail and went outside. He dug up a lot of slugs and earthworms. I looked at my watch. It was

11:00! School had started two hours ago! Mrs. Finkelplotz had probably called my mom by now to say I wasn't there. I was in big, big trouble!

Chapter 19

When the pizza guy came back inside, he was carrying a pail full of slippery, squirming things. It made me want to puke.

The pizza guy looked pretty close to puking himself. He made up six pizzas with the slugs and earthworms and shoved them into the oven on a large wooden paddle.

"MMMM," slurped the littlest zombie. "THAT SMELLS YUMMY."

I didn't think it smelled yummy. I thought it smelled pukey.

When they came out of the oven, the pizzas stank up the whole place and looked even worse. But the zombies didn't seem to mind. They

gobbled them right up. All six of them. They actually liked the taste.

"PIZZA GOOD," said the littlest zombie. He belched loudly.

"PIZZA ALMOST AS GOOD AS HUMAN BRAINS," said the head zombie. He took a table cloth and wiped the hole in his face that would have been his mouth if he had lips.

"O.K.," said the pizza guy, going to the cash register. "With tax, six pizzas comes to eighty-seven dollars and fifty-three cents."

I looked at the head zombie. "I sure hope you guys brought along some money with you,"

"ZOMBIES NEVER CARRY MONEY," declared the head zombie.

"Really?" I asked. "Why not?"

"NO POCKETS."

I turned to the pizza guy. "The zombies don't seem to have any money with them."

The pizza guy's eyes bugged out.

"Whatta you mean they don't have any money?" he sputtered. "I made them six pies, pal. Six disgusting pies with slugs and earthworms. If they can't pay me, then *you* better."

"All I've got on me is my lunch money," I said. "And that's only three dollars."

The pizza guy was getting pretty upset. His face was red and he was breathing hard.

"If somebody doesn't pay me soon," he threatened, "I'm calling the cops."

"It's fine with me if you call the cops." I turned to the head zombie. "O.K. with you guys if he calls the cops?"

"TOTALLY O.K.," agreed the head zombie.

"ARE COPS GOOD TO EAT?"

"I don't think so," I said.

Breathing even harder, the pizza guy picked up his phone and dialed. After a few rings, somebody must have answered.

"Yo, this is Vinnie at Original Rocco's on Broadway," said the pizza guy into the phone. "I got a bunch of zombies here who refuse to pay me for six pizzas. How soon can you get over here and arrest them?"

The person on the other end must have asked him a question.

"Zombies," repeated the pizza guy into the phone. "Z-O-M-B-E-E-S. You know, the un-dead? Bare feet, white eyes, skin peeling away in long strips?"

I heard a dial tone blast out of the phone. The pizza guy's face was almost purple with rage.

"The cops hung up on me," he griped. "Do you

believe that?"

I shook my head. "Boy, what is this city coming to when cops won't arrest zombies for refusing to pay for pizza?"

Chapter 20

"You gotta pay me, kid," the pizza guy demanded.

"Wish I could, pal, but no can do." I smiled. "I mean that sincerely."

I turned to leave. With a roar of rage, the pizza guy rushed out from behind the counter and grabbed me by the shirt.

The pizza guy was the size of a mountain gorilla. I suddenly got a really bad headache.

The zombies moved toward us in their weird stiff-legged walk. They had us surrounded. Whooh! They sure smelled terrible. It wasn't just pizza-with-slugs-and-earthworms-breath smell, either. The pizza guy let go of me.

The head zombie picked up the pizza guy by his collar and dangled him up in the air. I must say, he was pretty strong for a dead guy. The pizza guy trembled. The head zombie turned to me.

"TELL ME, DANNY, DID YOU LIKE BEING GRABBED BY YOUR SHIRT?" he bellowed.

"Not so much," I said.

The head zombie turned to the pizza guy he

was dangling two feet off the ground.

"DANNY DID NOT LIKE BEING GRABBED BY HIS SHIRT," he roared. "DANNY IS A GOOD FRIEND OF OURS. IF YOU APOLOGIZE TO HIM, MAY- BE WE WILL NOT TAKE YOU BACK TO THE GRAVEYARD FOR A BETWEEN-MEAL TREAT."

The pizza guy nodded like a bobble-head doll.

"I'm s-sorry I g-grabbed you by your sh-shirt," he stammered.

"HOW SORRY?" demanded the head zombie.

"V-very s-sorry," stuttered the pizza guy.

"SORRY ENOUGH TO GIVE US SIX PIZZA PIES WITH PEPPERONI, SLUGS, AND EARTHWORMS FOR FREE?" shouted the head zombie.

"You m-mean the six p-pies you just ate?" he asked.

"YES," roared the head zombie. "AND SIX MORE TO TAKE WITH US."

The pizza guy did his bobble-headed nodding again.

"GOOD," howled the head zombie. "WELL, DANNY, IT WAS NICE MEETING YOU. WE THANK YOU FOR INTRODUCING US TO PIZZA."

He held out his hand for me to shake.

I looked at his hand. The fingers were kind of greenish, rotting and squooshy. The thought of touching them made me want to hurl my guts out. But I didn't want to hurt his feelings. I grabbed his hand and shook it fast, then wiped my hand on my jeans.

"NEXT TIME YOU ARE IN THE NEIGHBORHOOD," urged the head zombie, "DROP BY THE GRAVEYARD AND SAY HELLO. WE WILL TALK ABOUT

OLD TIMES."

"O.K., thanks," I said. "Maybe I'll do that."

"THAT WAS A SERIOUS INVITATION," he shouted.

"O.K.," I said.

"IF YOU DO NOT VISIT US SOON," he added, "WE WILL COME AND VISIT *YOU.*"

Chapter 21

I ran the rest of the way to school. When I got there, I raced up the steps.

I could just imagine the expression on Mrs. Finkelplotz's face when I told her why I was late today. But she had to forgive me when she heard my excuse. Yeah, right. She was really going to love my excuse.

When I got to my classroom, I was all out of breath. My clothes were dirty, my shoes were muddy, and I was a mess. I looked at my watch. It was 11:30. I was two and a half hours late for school!

With my heart hammering so loudly that anyone could hear it, I opened the door to the classroom.

It was geography time. Mrs. Finkelplotz had her hand on a big blue globe of the world. When I walked into the classroom, Mrs. Finkelplotz stopped talking, spun the big blue globe, then stared at me. All the kids in the class stared at me.

"Well, well, well," said Mrs. Finkelplotz. "Look

what the cat dragged in."

"I'm sorry I'm late, Mrs. Finkelplotz," I gasped, still out of breath. "But I have a really good excuse this time."

"I'm sure you do, Daniel," she said. "Does your excuse explain why you are two and one half hours late?"

"Yes, ma'am," I said. "It does."

"Well, then," she sighed, "go ahead. Let's hear it."

"O.K.," I said, "here goes. First I had to escape a bunch of zombies I ran into at the grave-yard who hadn't eaten in eighty years. They wanted me to take them to a restaurant that serves human brains. I ran away from them, but as I was passing Belmont Harbor, a pirate captain wanted to steal my lunch money. I ran away from him, too, but then a troll wanted me pay eighty thousand dollars to cross her bridge, and I had to remove a thorn from her paw and scare off three really rude billy goats by calling them Cow Tushy, Marmalade Fart, and Doody Breath."

I stopped for a breath.

"After that I ran into the pirate captain again, and this time he forced me onto his pirate ship, where I helped the pirates choose a new pirate captain and promise to stop being pirates and take tourists on cruises of the Chicago waterfront instead. And finally, I ran into the zombies again and they forced me to take them to Original Rocco's and stay with them till they were through eating six pizza pies with slugs and earthworms."

Mrs. Finkelplotz and the kids were very quiet for awhile. "That's a truly amazing story, Daniel," said Mrs. Finkelplotz finally.

"I'm glad you believe me, Mrs. Finkelplotz," I said.

"I didn't say I believe you," snapped Mrs. Finkelplotz. "I said, that's a truly amazing story.

What I would like you to do now is go home, get your mother, and bring her back here for a serious conference with Principal Under-pence at 3:00 p.m. when school is out. Do you understand me, Daniel? Say yes or no."

"Yes, Mrs. Finkelplotz," I said.

Chapter 22

"I knew it!" shouted my mother. "Danny, what did I tell you? Did I say 'If you're late again, I'm going to have to go to see Mrs. Finkelplotz?' Did I say that or didn't I?"

"You did, Mom," I admitted, "but you see —"

"And is that what happened or isn't it?" insisted my mother.

"It is, Mom," I said, "but the thing is —"

"What if Mrs. Finkelplotz sends you to Principal Underpence's office?" she asked.

"Um, I guess that could happen," I mumbled.

"What if Principal Underpence suspends you for being late so many times? What if you get kicked out of school altogether? What will happen

to you then? You won't ever be able to go to college or get a job or get married or have children. Do you want me to go through life without grand-children?"

"I guess not," I said.

"Then what can you do to avoid that?"

"I'm not sure," I admitted, "but I know some people who might be able to help me."

"Who can possibly help you now?" wailed my mother.

"Come with me and I'll show you," I said.

Chapter 23

When Mom and I arrived at the harbor, she seemed puzzled.

"Why have you brought me to Belmont Harbor?" she asked.

"I wanted you to meet some new friends of mine," I explained.

I guided Mom onto the dock. The waves were still slapping the hulls of the boats. The ropes were still clanking against the masts. We walked along the dock to the pirate ship. The Jolly Roger flag with its skull and cross bones was still flying from the top of the tallest mast.

"What on earth is this?" gasped my mother. "Why, it looks like a pirate ship!"

"That's what I've been telling you," I said.

The pirate with the parrot on her shoulder was high up in the rigging. She was taking the Jolly

Roger down and replacing it with the City of Chicago flag.

"Ahoy there!" I shouted.

The pirate turned around and looked down at us. Then she held a spyglass up to her eye.

"Danny, is that you, lad?" she hollered.

"Aye, aye!" I yelled. "Permission to come aboard?"

"Permission to come aboard granted!" she shouted.

Other pirates came to the railing of the deck and starting waving and calling my name.

"Danny, these pirates seem to know you," my mother whispered.

"They do know me, Mom," I said. "I met them this morning on the way to school. Come aboard the ship. I want you to meet them."

"B-but they're p-pirates!" she stammered.

"Not anymore they're not," I said.

When Mom and I went aboard the ship, Tiny Tom and all the other former pirates gathered around us. They were thrilled to meet my mom. You could tell she was pleased. And when I said I needed their help, they were only too glad to say yes.

"They're so polite," Mom whispered. "I had no idea pirates were so polite."

Chapter 24

I took Mom and the pirates to the bridge. Throg clambered out of the water and almost made my mother jump right out of her skin.

She screamed. Throg screamed. Then all three of us screamed.

All the pirates, led by Tiny Tom, walked onto the bridge after us.

"This is a troll bridge!" Throg shouted. "If you people want to cross this bridge, you have to pay a troll a toll! Eighty thousand dollars apiece!"

"Hey, Throg!" I yelled. "It's me, Danny. I was here only a few hours ago. Don't you remember me?"

"Danny!" Throg shrieked. "Have you brought

the chocolate ice cream and sprinkles with chocolate whipped cream and a maraschino cherry?"

"No, Throg," I said. "I haven't had a chance to get anything yet. I came because I need your help."

"You need my help?" hooted the troll. "Who's going to help me? I've got a thorn in my paw!"

"I already took the thorn out of your paw," I

said. "Don't you remember?"

Throg scratched her head. Then she looked at her paw.

"You're right," she admitted. "The thorn is gone."

"So will you help me?" I asked.

"I guess so," she agreed. "But only if you can grant me a wish."

"We've been through all that already," I sighed.

Chapter 25

When Throg, the pirates, my mother, and I got to the graveyard, it was even foggier than it had been in the morning. The tops of the gravestones peeked through a blanket of whitish gray fog that covered the ground. A chill wind groaned through the trees. I could tell Mom was pretty spooked.

"Danny, what are we doing in a cemetery?" she whispered to me.

"I wanted you to meet some more people I know, Mom," I said.

"More strange friends of yours?" she hissed.

"Not friends, exactly," I said. "But they're not so bad once you get to know them. Once you get past the smell."

"Are these not-exactly-friends of yours…alive?" she whispered.

"Not exactly," I said.

Just then a zombie poked his head out of the blanket of fog. A lot of the skin was missing from his face, and one eyeball was kind of hanging out of an eye socket. Mom screamed. I screamed. Throg screamed. Then all of the pirates screamed, even Tiny Tom. That scared the zombie, and

so he screamed. It was a pretty terrible sound, I tell you.

Then the head zombie poked his head out of the fog blanket, and everybody screamed all over again.

"DANNY, IS THAT YOU?" howled the head zombie.

"Yes, it is," I said. "You said to come back and visit you, so here I am. And I've got a favor to ask you."

"YOU WANT ME TO PICK SOMEBODY UP BY THE COLLAR AND TWIST HIS HEAD AROUND A FEW TIMES?" he shouted.

"Not exactly," I said.

Chapter 26

We arrived at the school a little early. It was only 2:45, not 3:00, but we decided to go upstairs anyway. Counting me, Mom, Throg, the pirates, and the zombies, there were more than fifty of us.

I knocked on the door of Mrs. Finkelplotz's classroom.

"Come in!" called Mrs. Finkelplotz.

So I walked inside.

"Ah, Daniel," said Mrs. Finkelplotz when she saw me. "You're a little early, but that's all right. Did I or did I not tell you to bring your...? Oh, hello," she said when she saw my mother. "I'm glad you could come, Mrs....

EEEEEEAAAAGGGHHHHH!"

That's when Throg walked into the class-room, followed by the zombie leader. Tiny Tom and most of the pirates and zombies squeezed in behind us.

All the kids in the classroom leaped out of their seats and flattened themselves on the farthest wall where the windows were, along with Mrs. Finkelplotz. Their mouths were wide open, but no sound was coming out of them. Their eyes were popping out of their heads.

"Good afternoon," I said. "Mrs. Finkelplotz, you didn't believe me when I told you why I was late for school today, so I brought all the people I told you about to prove I was telling the truth. Now that they're here, do you have any questions

you want to ask them?"

Mrs. Finkelplotz was frozen in place.

"I said, do you have any questions you want to ask them, Mrs. Finkleplotz?"

Mrs. Finkelplotz shook her head from side to side.

"So that's a No?" I pressed.

She nodded her head up and down.

"Good," I said. "So does that mean you believe what I told you about why I was late for school today?"

She nodded her head violently up and down.

"And do you believe what I told you the other times I was late for school?"

She nodded her head even more violently up and down again.

"Is there anything at all you'd like to say now, Mrs. Finkelplotz?"

Mrs. Finkelplotz tried to speak, but it came out as a hoarse and stuttery whisper:

"T-tell them to g-go away."

"I will tell them to go away," I agreed. "But only if you say 'I will never doubt you again. I will believe whatever you tell me, no matter how crazy.'"

"If you t-tell them to g-go away," she stammered, "I will n-n-never doubt you again. I will b-b-believe whatever you t-tell me, no m-m-matter how c-c-crazy."

"Thanks, Mrs. Finkelplotz," I said. I turned around to face all my new friends.

"And are there any questions you guys want to ask?"

"YES," roared the zombie leader. "ARE FINKELPLOTZES AS TASTY AS PIZZA WITH PEPPERONI, SLUGS, AND

EARTHWORMS?"

Mrs. Finkelplotz fainted. Luckily, Tiny Tom knew first aid and he was able to bring her out of it.

P.S. I don't know why, but for some reason, since that day I have never been late for school. Which is a shame, because now Mrs. Finkelplotz would believe me.